For Charlotte and Jake

First published 2017 by Walker Books Ltd
87 Vauxhall Walk, London SE11 5HJ

2 4 6 8 10 9 7 5 3 1

The right of Alex Milway to be
identified as the author and illustrator
of this work has been asserted by him in
accordance with the Copyright, Designs
and Patents Act 1988

This book has been typeset in Burbank Big Regular

Printed in China

British Library Cataloguing in Publication Data:
a catalogue record for this book is available from the British Library

ISBN 978-1-4063-4606-0

www.walker.co.uk

PIGSTICKS AND HAROLD

LOST IN TIME!

Alex Milway

WALKER
BOOKS

The Rubbish Spaceship

The Tuptown Science Fair started in an hour, and Pigsticks was beginning to worry. He was trying to make a spaceship for the Best Invention competition, but so far all he'd made was a mess.

Harold had told him that everyone else had already prepared their inventions.

PIRATE GEORGE'S DIVING SUIT

For formal underwater occasions.

BOBBINS'
(THE ANGRY MOUSE)
CALMING SALTS

Never be angry again!
(Unless something really annoying happens.)

ALICE ANTEATER'S ROBOTIC BUTTERFLY FEEDER

Spoil butterflies from the comfort of your sofa!

SISSY PORCUPINE'S GIANT CARROT

For when you really need to see in the dark!

EVIE BIRD'S INFLATABLE TREE

Ideal for the bird on the go.

OTTERLY'S PORTABLE LIGHTHOUSE

Never leave a dangerous rock unlit.

BONZO'S SUPER HAMMER

For when you have too many nails and too little time.

BENJAMIN HORSE'S MEGA-LOUD GUITAR

Everyone will listen to your music! (They won't have a choice.)

HAROLD'S BEST-EVER BATTENBURG CAKE

Scientifically proven to be extra pink and delicious.

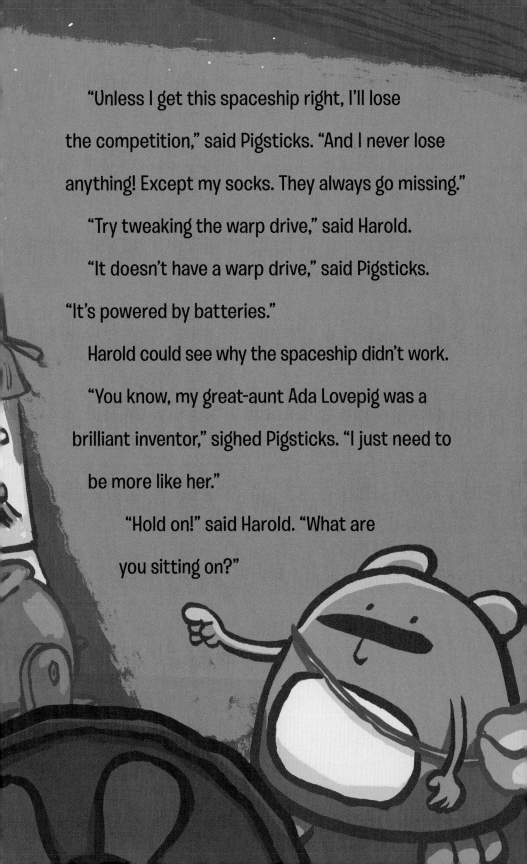

"Unless I get this spaceship right, I'll lose the competition," said Pigsticks. "And I never lose anything! Except my socks. They always go missing."

"Try tweaking the warp drive," said Harold.

"It doesn't have a warp drive," said Pigsticks. "It's powered by batteries."

Harold could see why the spaceship didn't work.

"You know, my great-aunt Ada Lovepig was a brilliant inventor," sighed Pigsticks. "I just need to be more like her."

"Hold on!" said Harold. "What are you sitting on?"

Pigsticks looked at his seat. It was covered in dials and switches and what he'd thought was an arm rest was actually a lever. Carved on the front were the words *LOVEPIG TIME MACHINE*.

WARNING: VERY RUSTY AND FRAGILE!

-65000000

LOVEPIG TIME MACHINE

LOVEPIG
TIME MACHINE

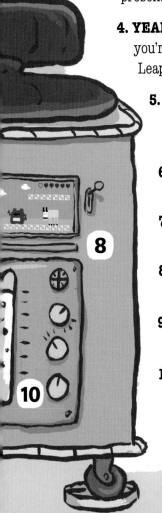

1. PADDED BOTTOM PROTECTOR A comfy seat. Fits mammals and reptiles. Not suitable for fish.

2. INTER-DIMENSIONAL TIME COGS Old-fashioned but effective at keeping the hands of time turning.

3. HOME-TIME DISPLAY Never miss a party in the present — keep one eye on the home-time clock.

4. YEAR DISPLAY Shows the exact point in time you're travelling to — responds to the Quantum Leap Lever.

5. ON/OFF SWITCH If the time machine doesn't work, try turning it off and on again.

6. THE SPACE BRACE A supportive back rest to keep you upright during time hops.

7. QUANTUM LEAP LEVER Pull this to set your desired time period destination.

8. TRAVEL GAMES For passing the time as you pass through time.

9. EMERGENCY OVEN For time periods without kitchens — or food.

10. VORTEX BATTERY Works in any conditions, guaranteed to last long into the future, and far into the past.

"A time machine?" cried Harold, stepping back in case he disappeared into the past.

"Great-aunt Ada must have made it!" said Pigsticks. "This was her workshop! She was a genius. She invented boarband internet and spam mail, too – but then everyone makes mistakes."

Harold looked at the time machine. "Do you think it actually works?" he said. "It's very old..."

"Let's see," said Pigsticks. He pressed a switch and a bright yellow light flickered on. He was so excited that his tail curled into a ball.

"Success!" he cried. "The Best Invention prize will be mine! We can use the time machine to go into the future and learn how to build a real spaceship."

"We?" said Harold.

"There are two seats," he said. "Perfect for a time traveller and his assistant!"

"But I'm happy in the present," said Harold. "Anyway, this is a terrible idea. Look how rusty that time lever is."

"We can't let a bit of rust stand in our way!" cried Pigsticks. "If we travel through time, we'll be legends! They'll talk about us for ever!"

Harold didn't want to be talked about for ever.

"But Harold," said Pigsticks, "think of the cakes!"

"Cakes?" said Harold. He wasn't sure what cakes had to do with time travel, but he was definitely interested all the same.

"Yes!" said Pigsticks. "Imagine all the future cakes that no one's invented yet, and all the ancient cakes that no longer exist!"

Harold imagined the cakes. They were delicious.

"So," said Pigsticks, "are you coming?"

"Hang on," said Harold, grabbing his bag. "We'll need my Best-Ever Battenburg for the journey."

MOLECULE MERINGUE

A fizz-whizzer of a sponge pudding, filled with buzzing protons and topped with tongue-popping sugary electrons.

GREAT PYRAMID CAKE

A triple-decker gateau, filled with strawberry jam and cream. Topped with a lone strawberry for good measure.

CAKEHENGE

A structural treat, built with fresh cream eclairs, topped off with lashings of chocolate.

Harold took his seat on the time machine and held on tight.

"To the future!" cried Pigsticks.

"To the cakes!" cried Harold.

Pigsticks pulled the lever. There was a clunk and a crack.

"Er – Pigsticks?" said Harold, as the world began to blur. "Was the lever meant to break off in your hand?"

CRACK!

Stuck In Time

VWORP! VWORP!

Travelling through time was a lot like falling down a very large, very scary plughole. Pigsticks and Harold span in circles as history flashed before their eyes. Then, with a thud, the machine stopped.

"This doesn't look like the future," whispered Harold. "This looks like..."

"The time of the dinopigs!"

"We're in the past," said Pigsticks. "How interesting."

"It's not interesting. It's terrifying!" whispered Harold, edging away from a Tyrannosaurus Pig. "And the time machine is broken! We can't control where we travel to without the lever! How will we ever get home?"

"We need to find something to replace the broken lever," said Pigsticks. "What about that stick?"

He pointed to a branch lying in a pile of dinopig eggs. "You fetch it. I'll guard the time machine."

"If you think so..." said Harold, reaching out.

Harold leapt onto the time machine, empty-handed. "Quick!" he cried. "Let's get out of here!"

Pigsticks gave the machine a thump and soon they were spinning through time. "Wherever we end up, it'll be better than here," he said, as they crash-landed again. But Pigsticks was wrong.

"We're in Ancient Egypt!" cried Harold.

"What a wonderful view," said Pigsticks, as they slid down a pyramid. "This must be the reign of..."

"Cleopigtra!" said Pigsticks. "And there she is!"

"How dare you use my favourite pyramid as a slide!" cried Cleopigtra, waving a scary-looking staff at them. "It's covered in pure gold!"

"And very tasteful it is too," said Pigsticks.

"We're very sorry," said Harold. And then he realized – Cleopigtra's staff would be the perfect replacement for the broken time lever...

"Pigsticks," he hissed. "The staff."

"A giraffe?" said Pigsticks, his ears a bit clogged from time travelling.

"No! Cleopigtra's stick," said Harold.

"She feels sick?" said Pigsticks.

"What are you two muttering about?" asked Cleopigtra, her eyes narrowing.

"We were wondering, your … royalness," said Harold. "Could we please borrow your staff?"

"HOW DARE YOU!" roared Cleopigtra. "Only a pharaoh can touch this staff. It belonged to Pigothep the Third. Guards! Lock them up!"

"Quick, Harold," whispered Pigsticks. "Get on. Let's get out of here!"

Pigsticks and Harold jumped backwards and forwards through time. Everywhere they looked for something to replace the broken time lever, but they had no luck.

There was nothing in London, where they got a nice warm welcome – a bit too warm for Harold's liking.

Then they visited New York City, but they didn't hang around for long.

Look, Harold! The Statue of Pigerty!

They bumped into Julius Squealer and found themselves at the sharp end of the law in Ancient Rome.

Harold was starting to feel time-travel sick.

"Isn't history exciting?" said Pigsticks.

"In books, yes," said Harold. "In real life, it's downright dangerous. And I haven't eaten a single cake yet. I just want to fix our time machine and get back home..."

He screwed his eyes up tight as the time machine landed again – on something soft...

FLUMPF

"This place looks rather nice!" said Pigsticks.

"I'm not so sure," said Harold. "I can see some very

angry-looking boats..."

"Oh, nonsense," said Pigsticks. "I have a good

feeling this time. The air's clear,

the view is stunning—"

"And the time machine is

sinking!" cried Harold.

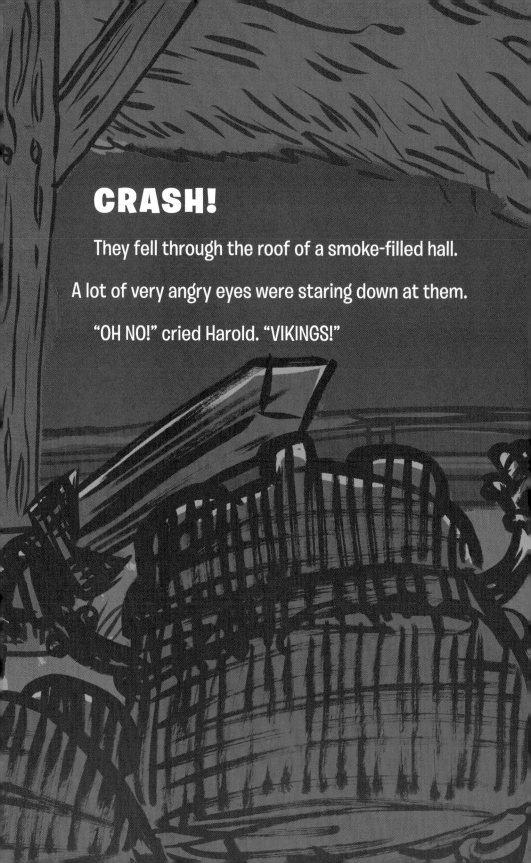

CRASH!

They fell through the roof of a smoke-filled hall.

A lot of very angry eyes were staring down at them.

"OH NO!" cried Harold. "VIKINGS!"

The Viking chief stormed up to them, waving her terrifying axe.

"She doesn't look happy," whispered Harold.

"Quite the opposite," whispered Pigsticks.

"I am Hamfrida, Chief of the village!" she cried. "You fell from the sky on your silver throne and ruined our midsummer party!"

Harold felt terrible. There was nothing worse than someone ruining your party, especially if you hadn't had cake yet. "We're ever so sorry," he said.

"You will pay for this!" growled Hamfrida.

"But we don't have any money!" said Pigsticks.

"We don't want your money," said Hamfrida. "We will take your freedom! We will burn your silver throne to celebrate midsummer, and banish you to the ice lands ... FOR EVER!"

"FOR EVER?" said Pigsticks.

"FOR EVER!" said Hamfrida.

"For ever is a very long time," said Harold.

"And it starts RIGHT NOW!" said Hamfrida.

"No it doesn't!" said Pigsticks. He grabbed Harold's hand and they ran into the Viking village.

The streets were littered with stinky dried fish and the vicious Vikings were everywhere, tossing axes at them and shouting scary words.

Soon they were trapped in a dead-end.

"Pigsticks," said Harold. "This is the end of the road. It's been nice knowing you..."

The Vikings grabbed them and tied them up tightly.

"They're going to destroy our time machine," said Harold, as the Vikings prepared their bonfire. "We'll be stuck in the past for ever!"

"Don't be silly," said Pigsticks. "We are Pigsticks and Harold! We're too important to spend our lives in an icy wasteland. There must be a way out."

Harold tried to cheer himself up.

"At least we still have my Battenburg cake," he said. "Would you like a piece?"

"Harold," said Pigsticks, "this is not the time for cake!"

Cake ... or Doom!

As night fell, the Vikings lit the bonfire.

"This is it," said Harold. "Our future's about to go up in flames."

"Nonsense!" said Pigsticks. "It's our past that's going up in flames. We have a very bright future."

But he didn't sound very certain.

Harold watched in silence as the Vikings carried the time machine towards the fire.

"There's something very familiar about these Vikings," said Pigsticks. "They're very strong for their size. Almost as strong as you, Harold..."

"They're nothing like me," said Harold.

At that very moment, Hamfrida slipped on a dried fish. She tumbled to the ground and her helmet fell off...

"She's a hamster!" cried Harold. "She *is* like me!"

"I thought as much!" said Pigsticks. "Everyone knows that hamsters take parties very seriously."

And then Harold had an amazing idea. "Pigsticks!" he cried. "Cake!"

"I already said no."

"No! I mean, hamsters love cake. And there wasn't any cake at the Vikings' party. I'd have smelled it."

"Maybe cake doesn't exist yet?" said Pigsticks.

"You mean these hamsters have never tasted cake before?" said Harold. "No wonder they're so angry – a hamster without cake is a grumpy hamster!"

"The Battenburg is our only hope," said Pigsticks.

Harold cleared his throat. "Excuse me, Hamfrida," he said. "This looks like a very lovely party – but I have something that will make it even better."

Hamfrida turned towards him slowly. "HOW DARE YOU!" she said. "NOTHING could make my party better! I throw the best parties in HISTORY!"

"We've seen quite a lot of history, and you definitely don't," said Harold. "A party isn't a party without Battenburg cake."

Hamfrida was suspicious.

"What's Battenburg cake?" she said.

"Set me free and I'll show you," said Harold.

Hamfrida stared at Harold for a moment – and then she cried, "UNTIE THE PRISONER!"

Harold held out the Battenburg. Hamfrida took a sniff, then a bite. Everyone held their breath.

"This cake is so pink, yet so yellow ... so moist and delicious ... so stupendous ... it's THE FOOD OF THE GODS!" said Hamfrida.

She made all the Vikings try the Battenburg. They agreed it was the best thing they'd ever eaten – even better than dried fish.

"How can we ever reward you for the gift of cake?" said Hamfrida.

"Could we have our silver throne back, please?" asked Harold. "We need it to get home."

"Oh, but that wouldn't be a gift!" said Hamfrida. "There must be something else?"

"What we really need is something to replace the broken lever," said Harold. "Hamfrida ... please could we have your axe?"

"My axe? You're welcome to it," said Hamfrida.

Hamfrida then had a terrific thought. "And in return," she said, "maybe you could give us the recipe for your wonderful cake?"

"I'd be delighted!" said Harold. "What an honour!"

Once Harold had taught the Vikings to make Battenburg, Hamfrida handed over her golden axe. Harold fitted it into the time machine where the lever had been and set the time to the present day.

"But we need to go to the future," said Pigsticks.
"I need to build a spaceship so I can win the Best
Invention Prize at the science fair!"

Harold shook his head. "Absolutely not," he said.
"Some things are more important than winning
prizes. Like being alive, for instance."

And then Pigsticks said something Harold never
thought he'd hear him say: "You're right."

Pigsticks and Harold climbed onto the time
machine and each put a hand on the axe.

"Ready?" said Pigsticks. "One ... two ... three!"

Pigsticks and Harold crashed down in the middle of the science fair. Everyone in Tuptown was very surprised to see them.

"Where did you come from?" asked Milton.

"The past!" said Pigsticks.

"Rubbish," said Bobbins.

"It's true!" said Pigsticks. "We found this time machine in my attic and travelled through history!"

"Prove it!" said Bobbins.

"All right," said Pigsticks, standing up. "This, ladies and gentlepigs, is a genuine Viking axe."

"NO!" cried Harold.

"Don't touch it—"

Prove it!

But it was too late.

As soon as Pigsticks pulled the axe out, the time machine disappeared.

Harold was gone.

"Where is he?" asked Alice.

"He's lost in time," said Pigsticks. "He could be anywhere in history. And it's all my fault!"

"But what will we do without Harold?" cried Otterly. "Who'll make our birthday cakes for us?"

"Who'll water my garden when I'm on holiday?" said Alice, with tears in her eyes.

FITZz_z

"Who'll save the day when one of Pigsticks' ridiculous ideas goes wrong?" said Milton.

"He was my best friend," whimpered Pigsticks. "Harold won't survive out there on his own—"

Suddenly everything went dark. The room began to shake. Light shone through a crack in the door...

"What's that?" whispered Pigsticks.

Everyone rushed outside – and there, on Tuptown

Village Green, was a spaceship.

"Are they aliens?" asked Bonzo.

"Are we being invaded?" asked Sissy.

"Could it be—" said Pigsticks – but before he

could finish, a tiny astronaut started walking slowly

down the spaceship ramp.

The astronaut took off his helmet.

Everyone gasped.

It was Harold!

"You're back!" cried Pigsticks, overjoyed. "Where have you been?"

"Far into the future," said Harold. "And unlike the past, everyone was very friendly."

"That's a relief," said Pigsticks.

"I know," said Harold. "Anyway, some helpful moon hamsters showed me how to build a spaceship."

"And you did it all by yourself?" said Pigsticks.

"Yes, I suppose I did," said Harold proudly. "And this ship travels through time AND space!"

"You've been into space?" asked Milton.

"Of course I have," said Harold. "It's great, once you get used to endless silence and neverending darkness. Do you want to see for yourself?"

"Do we ever!" cried Milton. "But before we go, I have an announcement. I hereby declare that the prize for best invention goes to: Harold!"

"Me?" said Harold. "I never win anything."

"Although ... the spaceship was my idea, so I'm the winner really," said Pigsticks.

"I suppose you're right," said Harold.

"Let's go into space!" said Pirate George. "Power up the warp drive. It's time to..."

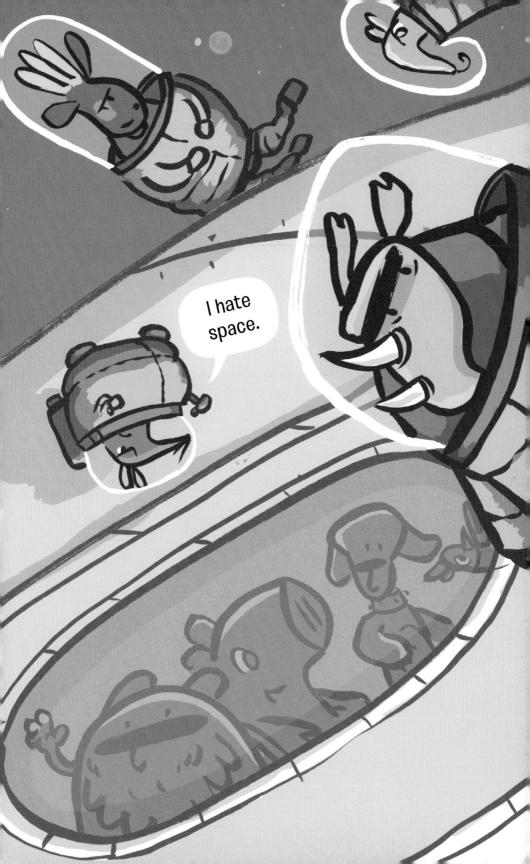

"What an adventure!" said Pigsticks. "I wonder where we'll end up next."

"I'd like to visit the Vikings again," said Harold. "I've got more cakes for them to try. Speaking of which, I brought this Atom Cake back from the future for you. Go on. Take a bite..."